FRIENDS and foes

poems about us all

DOUGLAS FLORIAN

Beach Lane Books   New York London Toronto Sydney New Delhi

To Henri Lallouz,
a sweet fellow!

BEACH LANE BOOKS • An imprint of Simon & Schuster Children's Publishing Division • 1230 Avenue of the Americas, New York, New York 10020 • Copyright © 2018 by Douglas Florian • All rights reserved, including the right of reproduction in whole or in part in any form. • BEACH LANE BOOKS is a trademark of Simon & Schuster, Inc. • For information about special discounts for bulk purchases, please contact Simon & Schuster Special Sales at 1-866-506-1949 or business@simonandschuster.com. • The Simon & Schuster Speakers Bureau can bring authors to your live event. For more information or to book an event, contact the Simon & Schuster Speakers Bureau at 1-866-248-3049 or visit our website at www.simonspeakers.com. • Book design by Ann Bobco • The text for this book was set in Gotham. • The illustrations were done with colored pencils and crayons on manila paper. • Manufactured in China • 0418 SCP • First Edition • 10 9 8 7 6 5 4 3 2 1 • Library of Congress Cataloging-in-Publication Data • Names: Florian, Douglas, author. • Title: Friends and foes : poems about us all / Douglas Florian. • Description: First Edition. | New York : Beach Lane Books, [2018] | Includes bibliographical references and index. • Identifiers: LCCN 2017042960 | ISBN 9781442487956 (hardback) | ISBN 9781442487963 (eBook) • Subjects: | BISAC: JUVENILE FICTION / Stories in Verse. | JUVENILE FICTION / Social Issues / Friendship. | JUVENILE FICTION / Humorous Stories. • Classification: LCC PS3556.L589 A6 2018 | DDC 811/.54—dc23 LC record available at https://lccn.loc.gov/2017042960

Contents

What Friends Are For

For sharing.
For caring.
For giving.
Forgiving.

For walking.
For talking.
For waiting.
Relating.

For pleasing.
For teasing.
For finding.
Reminding.

For lending.
For mending.
For treating you fair.
But what matters most?
For just being there.

I Like You

I like you when you listen.
I like you when you talk.
I like you when you whistle.
I like you when we walk.

I like you when we wrestle.
I like you when we race.
I like you when you tell a joke
or make a silly face.

I like you when we play all day.
Or when the play must end.
But **most** of all I like you
because you are my friend.

You Don't

You don't text.

You don't call.

You don't message me at all.

You don't email.

You don't write.

We don't talk, day or night.

You don't tweet.

You don't chat.

You don't joke or chew the fat.

Not one note

did you send.

Hey! What's up with you, my friend?

Old Friends

(a poem for two voices)

We're old friends.	That's what we are.
We're old friends.	We go back far.
We're old friends.	We're friends true and true.
We're old friends.	But just like new.
We're old friends.	I don't want to jinx it—

but I know what she thinks before she even thinks it!

Close Friends

We stick, we two, like glue, like glue.
We stick like thick molasses.
So close we are, we stick like tar
(and share one pair of glasses).

You Lied to Me

You lied to me.
I thought you were true.
I didn't expect that
from someone like you.
I thought you were honest,
a friend to be trusted.
But now that connection
is broken and busted.
You lied to me.
It hurt me to learn it.
If you want my friendship,
then you'll have to earn it.

I'm Friends with Trees

I'm friends with trees,

with bumblebees,

and every creeping creature.

I'm friends with stones,

and dinosaur bones,

but mostly Mother Nature.

15

Strangers

Once we two were strangers.
I found you somewhat strange.
But when I learned about you,
then things began to change.
We come from different cultures.
We speak a different tongue.
I come from California.
You grew up in Hong Kong.
The foods we eat are different.
Our clothes are different too.
We've got different religions.
I look different than you.
Once we two were strangers.
We seemed so far apart.
But now despite our differences,
we're both the same at heart.

Billy the Bully

Billy the bully
was mean and atrocious,
spiteful and frightful
and fiercely ferocious.
He loved to wreak havoc,
disturbing the peace—
till he was surprised by
a girl named Clarisse.

How Do You Say "Friend"?

In Spain they say "amigo."
The Danish word is "ven."
Italians say "amico."
In Afrikaans it's "vriend."

The Maltese say "habib."
While French folk say "ami."
The Irish word is "cara."
Swahili "rafiki."

In different countries friendship
may have a different name.
But though the spelling's different,
the meaning is the same.

We Used to Be Friends

We used to be friends.
But we drifted apart.
Don't mesh anymore.
Don't see heart-to-heart.
We used to be friends.
We drifted away.
Will we get back together?
Well, maybe someday.

Imaginary Friend

I'm thinking thoughts
concerning my
imaginary friend.
He really isn't real at all—
he's make-believe, pretend.

I talk to him at times when I
am lonely and I'm bored.
Or if I feel neglected, lost,
abandoned, or ignored.

He listens to my problems;
then he offers a solution.
He makes my fears all disappear
and clears up my confusion.

I'm thinking thoughts so thoroughly,
but I **just** had one quite scary:
Perhaps my friend is really real,
and **I'm** imaginary!

Moved

My best friend moved away last week—
the girl who lived next door.
And every day we used to speak.
She's not here anymore.
We'd share all of our secrets
and all our hidden dreams.
We'd bike around the neighborhood
and plan all sorts of schemes.
We'd read each other stories
and tell jokes all the time.
We were so close in nature,
it's like we were in rhyme.
We helped each other study,
preparing for a test.
She was good at history.
In science **I** was best.
My best friend moved away last week.
I miss her very much.
But we still speak
ten times a week—
we love to keep in touch!

I Hate Your Hair

I hate your hair.

I hate your eyes.

I hate your stare.

I hate your lies.

I hate your knees.

I hate your nose.

I even hate

your tiny toes.

I hate it how

you walk so slow.

But still

I'd **hate**

for you to go!

Hey! You!

Hey! You!
You wanna be my friend?
Yeah! You!
My friend until the end?
To do my chores
and open doors.
To walk my dog
and write my blog.
To scratch my toes
and blow my nose.
To sweep my room
with my big broom.
To fix my chair
and comb my hair.
To feed my cat
and find my hat.
To mop my floor,
go to the store.
To do my mending, stitching, sewing.

Hey! You!
Where are you going?!

Give and Take

I gave you a dollar.
You gave me a dime.
I gave you ten lemons.
You gave me one lime.
I gave you red rubies, blue sapphires, and gold.
But **you** only sneezed
and gave me your cold.

Jealous

I used to be jealous
of someone I knew.
Her hair was so shiny.
Her clothes always new.
She had all the answers.
Her grades were so high.
She never seemed nervous
or needed to cry.
Her manner was patient
when waiting her turn.
Her voice was so gentle,
not blaring or stern.
She never was lonely.
Had so many friends.
And always was busy
on all her weekends.
I use to be jealous
of someone I knew.
Till one day she told me,
"I'm jealous of **you**!"

Not Talking

Sally will not speak to Sam.

Sam won't talk to Jill.

Jill won't say a word to Joe.

Joe's ignoring Bill.

Bill is not so nice to Pam.

Pam is sore at Sue.

And **I** would tell you more, perhaps—

but **I** won't talk to **you**!

The Fabulous Five

We're the fabulous five

on the basketball court.

We're the fabulous five.

Shooting hoops is our sport.

We're the fabulous five.

We love playing together.

We're the fabulous five

even when it's bad weather.

We're the fabulous five.

That's our fabulous name.

We're the fabulous five—

but we lose every game!

I'm Better

(a poem for **two** voices)

I'm better at hiking.

I'm better at jogging.

I'm better at reading.

I'm better at riddles.

I'm better at walking.

We **each** can find something
but **I'll** never find a friend

I'm better at biking.

I'm better at blogging.

I'm better at weeding.

I'm better at fiddles.

I'm better at talking.

that better we do,
better than you!

My Smartest Friend

I have a friend who's brilliant.
She's so sophisticated.
Her knowledge is enormous.
And she's highly educated.
Her grasp of facts is awesome.
Her memory is massive.
Her mind is great to calculate—
in math she is impressive.
She really is reliable.
She never will complain.
She's flexible and pliable
and eager to explain.
And though she's not so beautiful
(I've many friends far cuter),
I can't complain
or tax my brain . . .
my friend is a computer.

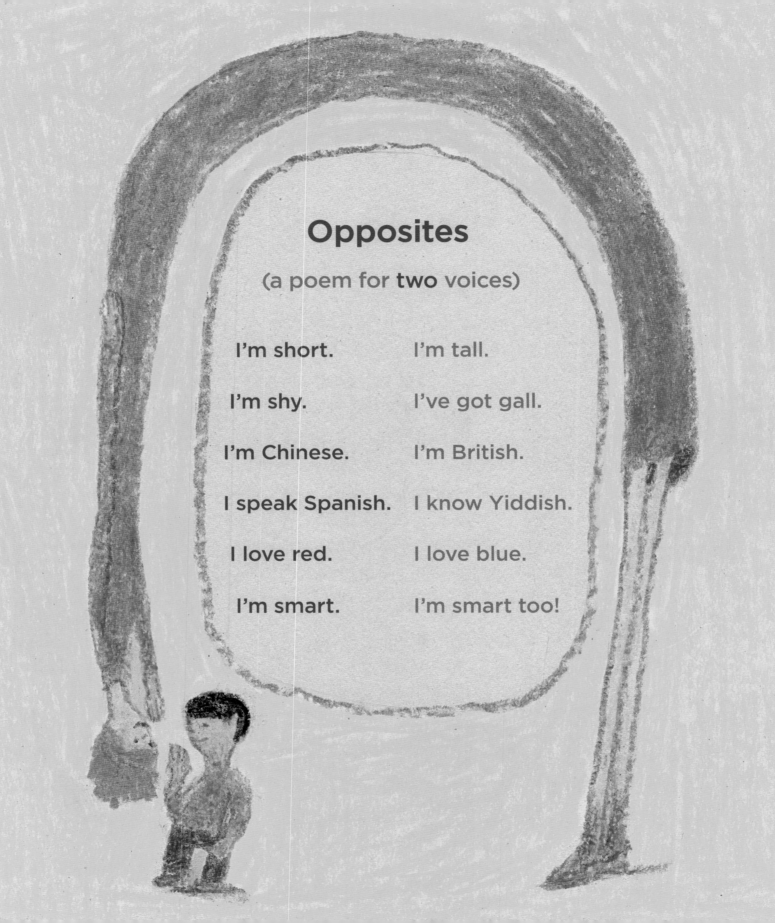

Opposites

(a poem for **two** voices)

I'm short.	I'm tall.
I'm shy.	I've got gall.
I'm Chinese.	I'm British.
I speak Spanish.	I know Yiddish.
I love red.	I love blue.
I'm smart.	I'm smart too!

Sleepover

Amy and Nomi and Dolly and Dotty
came to my home for a sleepover party.
We gabbed and we blabbed and we laughed and we leaped.
Had great tons of fun—but not too much sleep!

Friendship Is a Flower

Friendship is a flower.

You have to let it grow.

You really cannot rush it.

You have to take it slow.

Friendship is a flower.

You have to give it room

so it can grow the deepest roots

and marvelously bloom.